A Giant First-Start Reader

This easy reader contains only 32 different words, repeated often to help the young reader develop word recognition and interest in reading.

Basic word list for *Maxwell Mouse*

again	it	sweet
and	louder	that
bang	made	the
closer	Marsha	there
did	Maxwell	this
get	Mouse	tight
getting	noise	up
go	of	was
hear	see	what
home	sleep	who
is		you

Maxwell Mouse

Written by Sharon Gordon

Illustrated by Amye Rosenberg

Troll Associates

Library of Congress Cataloging in Publication Data

Gordon, Sharon.
    Maxwell Mouse.

    Summary: Just as he nears sleep, Maxwell hears
some disturbing sounds.
    [1. Sound—Fiction   2. Mice—Fiction]
I. Rosenberg, Amye.   II. Title.
PZ7.G65936Max   [E]   81-4653
ISBN 0-89375-501-X (case)   AACR2
ISBN 0-89375-502-8 (pbk.)

Home, sweet, home.

This is the home of Maxwell Mouse.

Sleep tight, Maxwell Mouse.

Bang! Bang! Bang!

Did you hear that?

What was that noise?

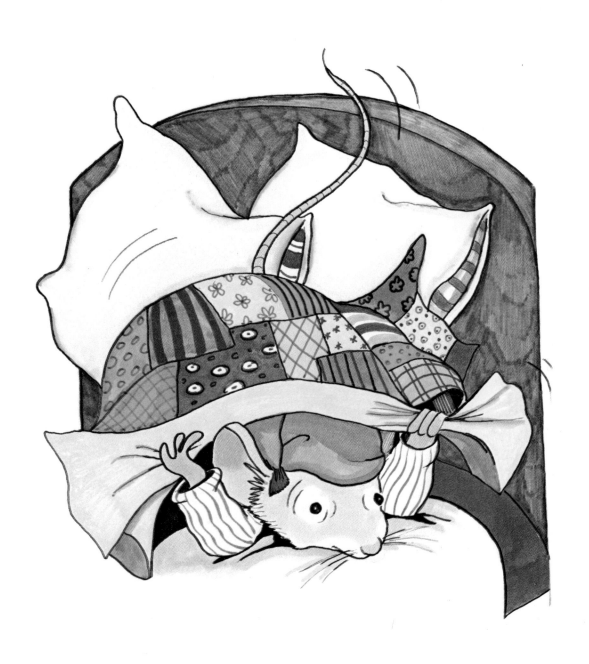

Who made that noise?

Get up, Maxwell Mouse.

Get up and see.

Bang!   Bang!   Bang!

There it is again.

It is getting louder.

The noise is getting louder.

What was it?

What was that noise?

Go and see, Maxwell Mouse.

Go and see who made that noise.

Bang! Bang! Bang!

There it is again.

It is getting closer.

The noise is getting closer.

What is it?

What is that noise?

There it is!

That is what it was.

Home, sweet, home.

This is the home of Marsha Mouse.

Sleep tight, Maxwell.

Sleep tight, Marsha.